THE REAPER'S MASK

To:Lizzie
enjoy Kam and
Eyden's Story ♡

Ky Venn

To: Lizzie
enjoy Kam and
Eyden's story ♡

THE REAPER'S MASK

A SHORT STORY

KY VENN

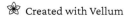

To the badass girlies who fall for the golden retriever boys.

I

KAMARI

1,068,516 souls taken.
1,068,516 humans I'd taken from their families.
1,068,516 lives tainted by Death.

I t never got easier. No matter how many I took. You would think I'd eventually get used to the essence of souls gracing my fingertips. The look in a person's eyes when the light finally left them. How it feels when their heart stops beating.

Granted, I hadn't been doing it that long. And one wouldn't think I was full of such darkness just looking at me. With my chocolate brown eyes and even darker hair, paired with a petite frame and the fact that I barely reach five feet tall, someone could take one look at me and think one of three things.

Innocence.

Child-like.

Weak.

Or maybe they would think all three. Unfortunately for

them, that couldn't be further from the truth. Inside my chest, where my soul once was, sits a heart as cold as ice and black as a starless night sky.

Technically I don't even have a heart anymore. I only have essence in my chest. The heartbeat was nothing but an illusion that came with the disguise I had to wear for three-hundred and sixty-four days of the year. It was part of my curse.

The curse that every grim reaper had to endure.

The same curse my father shouldered before me, only to pass it down to me upon his death.

My father loved me when he was alive, but no amount of love could have stopped him from having to give me this hateful curse. It was out of his control. *I blame the universe.* The same universe I blame for taking my father away from me in the first place. For putting an expiration date on the life of one who should be immortal. Five years ago he had hit his limit, and then passed the torch on to me. I hadn't had much time with him, but I was desperate to make him proud.

I only had an uncursed existence for eighteen years, and had been forced to work as Death for the last five.

Twenty-three years done. Four-hundred seventy-seven to go.

Eighteen glorious years in another realm, as my true self, with my family. Now I could never go back, I'd never see them again. Sometimes I wished I had never had those beautiful years. If you never have something, you don't even know what you're missing once it's gone.

Feels like I got the shit part of the bargain, if you ask me.

Because now I'm a prisoner with a life sentence.

2

EYDEN

It had been five years since Death had taken away my mother. Five years since I'd taken over the bookstore that was her pride and joy. Five years, and yet I still couldn't get my shit together long enough to get out of bed in the morning some days. Especially in the fall months when there was a permanent chill in the air, and all I wanted to do was stay under the covers with Phoenix, my long-haired cat whose fur was the darkest shade of black. But alas, duty called.

Most days I was able to get up because I knew that the bookstore I now owned was waiting for me, and that my mother would be rolling around in her grave if I didn't open it up and give the readers somewhere to escape their realities for the day.

In all honesty, I didn't mind running the bookstore. It gave me something to do, and peace and quiet to think when I needed it. Plus, who didn't love the smell of dusty old books?

Soon it would be Halloween, my least favorite day of the

3

year. The day Mom's cancer finally decided to steal her from me. I can still remember the rage I felt back then. Deep anger because I couldn't save her. That she was gone at only forty-four years old and had to suffer and wither away the last year of her life. That she'd never see me live out the rest of my life. I was only twenty-one. She had barely seen me live.

If I am being honest, I would say that the rage is still there, but I've had to come to terms with my loss. There's nothing I can do to bring her back. I know that no amount of pleading or begging would bring her back earthside to me.

With that thought, I pull back the covers and settle with the fact that I have to get out of bed today. Phoenix stays put, not budging at all.

"Must be nice to be a feline," I grumble to her. She slowly blinks her yellow eyes at me before closing them again and continuing her snooze.

I grab my ratty gray pullover from my closet and put on a pair of jeans before lacing my beat up black hightop chuck taylors on my feet. I take a look at myself in the mirror, run a hand through my blonde hair and call it a day before grabbing my backpack and keys and heading out the door.

3

KAMARI

I'd lived in Salem for the last five years and, I hated to admit it, back home paled in comparison to the beauty of Salem in the autumn. I still couldn't get over how every time I walked outside of my apartment I was assaulted with the yellow, orange, and reds of the changing leaves and the smell of apple cider and pumpkin pie spice that seemed to forever permeate the crisp air.

I missed my home, and my family, but these fall trimmings seemed to dull that ache some.

Previously I had never liked to stay in one place very long, but eventually I decided I needed to put my foot down and grow some roots.

Which was my first mistake.

Never get attached.

My second mistake was developing an unhealthy and unrealistic crush on the bookstore owner's son. They didn't even list a rule about that in the book on how to be a grim reaper. They just assumed I'd have enough common sense not to fall for a mortal who was unlikely to see the age of one hundred. But as soon as I'd entered the book store one fateful Tuesday morning in autumn and saw his face, the usual dead feeling inside me cracked for just a moment, and in leaked possibility.

A hint of joy.

A sprinkle of happiness.

He had been standing behind the counter, tending to another customer in front of him and paying me no mind. I took advantage of this fact and appraised him for a long while. His honey blonde hair was messy, which I soon found to be a usual occurrence, but simultaneously every piece looked like it was in place. His hazel eyes had a sparkle in them, which gleamed every time he smiled. Just thinking about his boyish grin gave me butterflies, *which shouldn't be possible*. But when it's a toothy grin that makes his dimple pop, it's hard for the impossible not to happen. His wardrobe rotated between a gray pullover, and a jean jacket with a t-shirt or flannel. He always wore light colored jeans and a pair of beat up old shoes.

How do I know so much about his appearance? *Because I've watched him.*

And why do I care? *That I still don't know.*

I shook myself out of my daydream, at the same time that he finished checking out his customer. Our eyes locked for just a moment before I broke the contact and disappeared into the shelves.

4

EYDEN

Just seeing her took my breath away. She'd been coming into the store for a while now, but she never ceased to blow me away whenever she walked through the door. Some days, I caught myself looking at the door whenever the bell would ding, hoping it would be her again. That the girl with unruly, curly brown hair, pale skin, and chocolate brown eyes would be gracing my store with her presence that day.

Back to reality, Eyden.

I finished giving the customer in front of me their change before attempting to make myself look busy by organizing the desk and the display shelf next to it – when in reality, I was watching the beautiful stranger peruse the horror section like she always did.

I wasn't sure if she ever noticed me or my watchful eyes, but if my mother could see me now she'd be doing a happy dance in her grave. Not because she was disappointed in me. No, she'd think my staring at the beautiful stranger would be an indication of a future between us. She'd tease me that I was getting old now, even though I was only twenty-five. She'd say I needed to settle down, get married, and have a couple kids.

I'm not saying she was wrong. I'm just saying my track record with women in the past didn't really scream stellar reputation.

I was a shy guy, who oftentimes was too nice to people for my own good. And most people would take advantage of it every time. I had a reputation for being a doormat – but it wasn't as if I could ever speak up and say anything about it. Instead, I just let it happen, and enjoyed the company while it lasted.

I made my way back behind the counter, and pulled out my old, worn copy of *Dracula,* and opened it to the dog eared page where I had last left off. Many probably have happier comfort novels, but I think those kinds of people don't realize that even in something portrayed as darkness, light and goodness can be found.

5

KAMARI

The town's only bookstore, The Cozy Cauldron, had a surprisingly decent sized horror section, despite its name sounding the complete opposite. I guess I shouldn't be too surprised, considering Salem's nickname is 'The Witch City.' Massachusetts as a whole was the Halloween capital of the United States. These people lived for Halloween and the fall season. So, of course their bookstores would be well-stocked with horror novels. I can't very well blame them for living for the one day of the year where the monsters can come out and play without fear of retribution.

When I say *monsters*, I don't mean criminal monsters. The murderers and what not.

No. I mean the witches, werewolves, vampires, and other beings who spend three-hundred-sixty-four days a year hiding themselves and then get to freely be themselves one night of the year. On Halloween, nobody questions whether we are wearing a costume or not. Everyone just assumes we are and compliments our badass costume making talent.

They don't realize that when they look at me on Halloween night, I could take their souls with the slash of my very real scythe.

I finger the spines of each book as I scan them on the shelves, looking for my comfort read. I lost my worn, written in, well-loved copy when I moved, and just never had the chance to get a new one to make my own.

It's a busy job being the Angel of Darkness.

Usually, when I move to a new town, I'll work my way through the local bookstore's horror sections, reading every book on the shelf. They were my only vice. Nothing could make me laugh like a good *horror* novel – because of how ridiculous they are. The same goes for horror movies. The predictability humans recreate us monsters with is laughable.

My finger finally stops on *Frankenstein,* and I pick it up without hesitation, eyeing the familiar cover and flipping through the pages. I could read it in one night with no shame. Replacing my annotations was going to be a pain in the ass though, but as many times as I'd read over my own scratchy written words in the margins, I'd have little trouble duplicating them.

I make my way back towards the front of the aisle and then over to the checkout counter. I stop just a few feet from the front of the shelf, and take a peek around the corner. Something twisted and curled in my stomach at the thought of seeing *him*. I'd never had this giddy feeling in my stomach before. Especially from just looking at a mortal. In my existence I had only ever been with other supernatural beings, which is a total different world of physical characteristics and sex techniques. Different sexual proclivities and opportunities for injury.

Dangerous sexual injuries.

My eyes land on golden blonde hair and those gorgeous hazel eyes, and it isn't until a few seconds of mindless staring that I realize those hazel eyes are looking right back into mine. I turn quickly, and feel my face heat at the fact that I've been caught.

But what makes it worth it is the small smirk I saw on his face before I turned.

He had been watching me too.

6

EYDEN

I can't help but smile when I'm graced with the sight of those familiar brown eyes peeking at me around the horror section bookshelf. It made me, once again, think of my mother. She would say this is a sign of potential love. But I won't get my hopes up. It's just a possibility. A possibility for friendship. A new connection, perhaps. I just couldn't let my pesky crush come to the surface or it could ruin the connection before it even started. We have never even spoken two words to each other – but as I watched her walk to the checkout counter, acting like nothing happened, I knew things were about to change.

"Find everything okay?" I asked as she handed me the copy of *Frankenstein* in her hands. Her nails were painted black, and it matched the outfit of black and gray she currently wore. There wasn't a pop of color about her, save for her ruby red lips and those brown eyes. But despite that, she still had a glow about her. Something warm emanating from deep within her. It's as if I could sense something lively behind her muted persona.

"Yup," she replied tersely. Her voice sounded like a melody as it tingled in my ears, despite her tone that leaned on the edge of annoyance. I didn't let it bother me as I scanned the barcode of her book and continued to ring up her purchase.

"That'll be $11.07," I said, my eyes connecting once more with hers. Up close, I could see a faint hint of green mixed within the brown, and it made my heart slam against my chest for no apparent reason.

What is wrong with me? I sound like a damn love sick puppy.

She pulled out her wallet and swiped her card quietly.

"Would you like a receipt?" I asked, my finger hovering above the 'no' button. She shook her head, and a small smile crept on my lips that I had guessed something correctly about her. She grabbed the book from my hands, and in doing so her fingers accidentally brushed mine. A small gasp escaped her lips, as an electrical wave of lightning went down my arm.

She looked into my eyes, as if to see what my reaction had been. If I'd experienced the same feeling. Her eyes broke away after only a moment, before she quickly grabbed the book and made her way towards the front door.

"Have a good day!" I yelled after her, but my words were lost to the wind, as she was already out the door.

7

KAMARI

I couldn't get that silly mortal's face out of my head. All we did was graze fingertips. Barely a breath of a touch, and my essence was screaming for more. Never before had I been affected in such a way. It made me almost physically ill. I wasn't supposed to be attracted to mortals. If nothing else, it made things messy. I was meant to live for hundreds of years. Their lifespans couldn't even touch mine. Falling in love with someone destined to die before you brought nothing but pain.

As I stepped out of the Cozy Cauldron, the townspeople were busy at work finishing up the decorations for Halloween the following night. They'd started weeks ago, but they always put up the finishing touches the night before, especially with the movie nights happening in the Common this night and the day after. They usually played *Hocus Pocus* and *Halloweentown* on Hallow's Eve, and then *Beetlejuice* and *Silence of the Lambs*. The scarier, less child friendly movies were always on Halloween, since the children and teenagers were walking around collecting their candy. It was a rotation every year of classic horror movies. Even though I somewhat hated them, I couldn't help but get sucked into movie night. I loved watching the characters on the screen. Sometimes they seemed so damn convincing. That, plus watching the mortals get frightened always gave me a laugh.

They sat, horrified by something on a screen when evil lurked just a few feet away from them.

Leaves of orange, red, and yellow littered the sidewalks, a few stray ones here and there blowing into the wind. The trees were almost bare this time of year, and the tree branches looked lonely and downright depressing hanging thereall gangly, naked, and devoid of life. Reminded me of Death. Reminded me of me.

It didn't take long for me to get back to my apartment. When I wasn't snagging the souls of the recently deceased, I made candles. I even owned a store that resided below my home. So in the eyes of anyone who came by, I looked like a real mortal – but I didn't do it to keep up my facade. I did it because I liked it. I liked mixing together the wax and putting new colors and scents together. Opening the door to my quaint little store and being pleasantly assaulted by different aromas was the highlight of my day. Not to mention, it passed the time. Not every day being a soul snatcher was busy, while others were so exhausting I would disappear into my apartment after, keep the shop closed, and sleep for days. Although I may not be a mortal, I still need, and cherish, my sleep.

I stuck the key inside the lock of my shop door, and jimmied the door knob as I always had to in order to get in, since the door loved to stick to the frame. I probably should have someone come out and take a look at it, but I had never gotten around to it. It just became part of my routine and a comfort in its own way.

I had recently stocked my shelves with all kinds of fall scents, preparing for Hallow's Eve and Halloween night. It was satisfying to come back in and see all of my hard work organized so nicely. There wasn't a bare spot on any of my shelves. Even though I, myself, would be busy the next two evenings, I typically hired someone part time to come in and handle things when I wasn't around. It was the closest I got to trusting a mortal – but I only had to entrust them with the store for two nights. All other times of the year if the store was closed, it was closed.

I made my way into the back room, and up the stairs to my apartment and then to my bed so I could get a few hours of sleep before heading over to the Common to people watch.

I have one night every year to myself, where I don't have to be collecting souls, and I will do everything I can to make sure it's the best night of the year.

8

EYDEN

I locked the doors and closed up shop early so I could make my way over to the Common for the annual movie night. Though excited, I groaned internally, because if I know anything, it's that Penelope will be there waiting for me.

There's nothing wrong with her, and when we dated a couple years back our relationship was fine, but we wanted different things out of life and I didn't want to waste anymore of my time in a relationship that wasn't going anywhere. We had remained friends after, but she was never shy about the fact that she still held love in her heart for me. It made things uncomfortable, but I did what I could to gently squash it down whenever it came up. There weren't a lot of people in town that I hung around with, so I didn't want to run off the one person I had left that could stand my mediocre existence.

I'm sure I seemed all warm, fuzzy, and meek on the outside, but on the inside I harbored anger and rage that I could do nothing about. Anger surrounding my mother's death. Anger at the world for taking her away. Anger for there not being a cure for cancer. Some days that grief hit me so hard I couldn't breathe. I'd walk into the Cozy Cauldron and want to turn right back around because I'd swear I could see her standing at the checkout counter, smiling at me and be devastated when she wasn't. Grief was a fickle little monster. It had no regard for responsibilities for plans, and strikes at any moment.

I had to take everything day by day and step by step – and my routine always seemed to stay consistent. The bookstore and then home. Home and then the bookstore. It didn't help that I rented the apartment right across the street. I didn't even get a scenic walk or drive every day. It was a five second sprint across the road. Nothing fancy, nothing different. Unless I went to the coffee shop next door and snagged something to keep me awake. That typically happened when I stayed up late the previous night reading a book, which was often.

But tonight was different. Tonight I would socialize.

I looked both ways before jogging across the street and took the five minute walk to the Common. From what I could see it was already starting to get packed with people. Everyone was excited to see movies we'd all seen a hundred times – but I couldn't complain about comfortability. Sometimes predictable was nice.

"Eyden!" A high-pitched voice said from a few feet in front of me. I looked up and my eyes found Penelope's blonde hair and blue eyes. She was truly gorgeous, and a small part of me wished we had worked out. That our relationship wasn't a dead end. She was a sweet Southern girl who wouldn't hurt a fly, who wanted six kids, a big ranch, and to move out of Massachusetts. I didn't mind the ranch, and I could get used to having that many children. It was the moving out of Massachusetts that was a dealbreaker for me. I couldn't leave the Cozy Cauldron behind. It was the only piece of my mother I had left. I would sell it when Hell froze over or over my dead body, but not a moment sooner.

"Penny," I replied, a warm smile on my face. I enveloped her in my arms, and breathed in her cherry scent. She was so familiar – so easy. I couldn't help the thought that entered my mind that maybe I had made a mistake. Maybe a future was in the cards for us.

But as I looked over her shoulder, and my eyes met a familiar pair of brown ones, the thought evaporated entirely.

9

KAMARI

It was a stupid idea to come here tonight.

When my eyes met his, I couldn't help the ache that formed in my heart, caused by seeing his arms around another woman. *Which is so stupid.* There is no possible way that it's written in the stars that I'm meant to have feelings for a mortal. There had to be another supernatural being out there that I was meant to love.

Someone who would live as long as I will.

Someone who would understand my job.

Someone who wouldn't fear my true form.

I quickly averted my eyes, breaking eye contact with him and making my way towards a booth that contained some form of strong alcohol. My eyes immediately leapt to a banner that read 'spiked apple cider.'

Perfect.

I pulled a twenty dollar bill out of my pocket and placed my order, throwing the change into the tip jar after I whispered to the girl to add in a little extra spice. As soon as my hand grasped the cup and I took a sip, I knew she had understood the assignment. I took a peek at her again and gave her a nod. She gave one in return, and then quickly got back to serving the people in the line before her.

The drink burned as it went down, from both the warmth of the liquid and the copious amounts of alcohol. But I wasn't complaining in the slightest. Anything to take the sudden edge off of my mood. That was the downside of moonlighting as a human every single day of the year but one. On Halloween, I got emotional. I got angry and sad. Happy and scared. I felt love and lust. I got hungry and tired. Just like any other human. Everything they felt and experienced, I did too. But if this was the price I had to pay to have even an ounce of normalcy, I'd take it.

I wasn't allowed to go *home*, which was a nice little sweet spot located between Earth and the Underworld. Its former title was the Otherworld. But it was Earth or the Underworld. No in between. I lost my family and my freedom the day the scythe was passed down from my father. I had no choice. My other siblings were far too young to even be considered a possibility. It's what you get when you're born into a supernatural family. Binding contracts and unachievable expectations. I'd never be as good as my father, but hell, I wasn't trying to be. This business got lonely. My dad may have preferred it that way, but I didn't. A soul could only be so lonely before it drowned in an ocean of isolation. And my soul didn't know how to swim.

10

EYDEN

I couldn't help but feel a pang in my chest when I watched the pained eyes of my beautiful stranger dart quickly away after seeing me hug Penny. It'd been half an hour since, and I still couldn't shake it. I could see her pinched expression in my mind, as if it was branded into my memory.

So maybe that's why my feet were suddenly carrying me towards where she stood, leaned against an oak tree, sipping a warm drink from a disposable cup. I was entranced by her and everything she did. It was like she had me under her spell, but I was by no means opposed to it.

"Hey," I said in a way of greeting after I had reached her. She was even more beautiful up close. The way her dark hair laid down her chest, and the way that her eyes sparkled even in the moonlight. The way she wore black clothing, dark eyeliner, and black nail polish. That the only color about her was her cherry red lipstick.

Mesmerizing.

"Hey," she replied, a wary look on her face. I can't blame her. We'd only seen each other in passing. I was a stranger.

"I'm Eyden," I held out my hand, and a zip of electricity went through my body as she put her small, soft hand into mine to shake.

"Kamari," she replied, our hands still joined. We both looked down and laughed, before she took her hand out of mine. "But you can call me Kam."

"It's nice to meet you, Kam," I said, attempting to keep my voice from becoming hoarse.

I can't believe I'm actually doing this. I'm actually talking to her.

There's a pregnant pause between us, in which we just keep stealing glances at one another. I knew I had to do something to fill the awkward silence, but I couldn't believe what came out of my mouth before I could stop it:

"Did you want to go out to dinner sometime?"

I watched as her eyes widened, as if she couldn't believe I just asked that either.

"I'm actually pretty busy the next few nights," she replied, her cheeks flushed pink. My heart sank, and I couldn't help but feel more embarrassed. "But, I don't have anyone to watch the movies with tonight, if you want to join me?"

I felt like a lovesick idiot when my heart pounded at her question. I gave her a small smile, way smaller than I actually wanted to or what reflected my happiness inside, before I gestured towards the lawn so we could find a spot to sit. She pushed off the tree she was leaning against, and I couldn't help but notice the redness her face still held, or the smile she had when she thought I wasn't watching.

II

KAMARI

There's no way this is going to end well.

I bicker back and forth with myself as I sit next to Eyden in the Common and wait for the movie to start rolling. There's a bag of popcorn and two pops between us, but his hand is so close to mine as he leans back and holds himself up that I could graze his fingers with just a slight shuffle of my own hand.

It's not fair for a mortal to be so handsome.

It's not fair for me to feel this way about a mortal.

Why the hell did I agree to this?

I tried to tell myself it was only one time. One date. If one could even consider this a date. But I knew it wouldn't just be one instance. We'd already hit it off so well that I knew he'd want to see me again. Things would never go back to how they were before. I wouldn't be able to walk into the Cozy Cauldron again no matter what happened – because in the end, I was inevitably going to have to break his heart. Before he grew old while I stayed young, and broke my own heart while I watched him fade away.

24

"Have you ever seen these movies before?" Eyden asked, popping a couple pieces of popcorn into his mouth. His voice was warm and deep. I could listen to him talk all day.

"No, I can't say that I have," I replied, taking a sip of my cola. I hadn't really watched many movies since taking up my job a couple years ago. I'd never paid much attention to what was playing on the screen when I watched the humans react to the "scary" parts of the movies. I was decently good at tuning out my surroundings. I tried to stay clear of anything that set unrealistic expectations in my mind. It's the same reason I avoided fantasy. Books and movies could end in happily ever afters all day long, but there wasn't a glimmer of hope for one in my lifetime.

"Well, you are in for a treat!" Eyden said enthusiastically. He made me want to give it a chance, and I didn't have much of a choice, for now anyway, seeing as it would be weird to walk away from him at this current moment. Not good first date etiquette.

Instead of giving him a verbal response, all I could do was smile at him. Maybe I should give things a try and say yes more often? Maybe I couldn't have a happily ever after, but I could at least have a happy midlife. A happy once in a while.

12

EYDEN

I laid in bed after movie night and couldn't stop staring at the ceiling. Phoenix was laying at my feet, sound asleep – man, I envied that feline. It was impossible for me to close my eyes and get even a wink of sleep. The only thing that was playing in my head was Kam's face. I feel like I hardly watched the movies. I watched her instead, waiting to see her reactions to some of my favorite childhood Halloween movies. Everytime she jumped or laughed it made me feel joy – until it made me think of my mother. I vividly remember watching them for the first time on the couch with my mom – with her fresh baked cookies and hot chocolate as a treat. But despite the pang of sadness I had, watching the girl I had a crush on smile and laugh at something I associated with such fond memories made it one of the best All Hallows Eve celebrations I'd had in a long time. It also topped any first date I'd ever had.

My mom would be so proud. Another wave of sadness washed over me.

It's such a bittersweet feeling when I think of her and our

memories together, but over time it's become a good kind of hurt. I can think of her without curling into a ball and sobbing. Instead the memories make me feel glad I got those times with her at all.

When the credits rolled, I had the strongest urge to kiss Kam's cherry red lips.

I wonder if her lips tasted like cherries.

I shook my head, because the last thing I should be thinking about in my empty bed and silent house was how her lips would feel on mine, and what she'd taste like.

13

KAMARI

I could hear the birds chirping outside my window, and I knew when I opened my eyes that it would be Halloween. That in just twelve hours or so, I would no longer have to moonlight as a mortal. No — I'd be able to spread my wings and be *free*. It was the one night a year I looked forward to. What I craved and hungered for all year long. Even if I had to spend most of the day still in my disguise, and I only got a few hours to be my true self it was worth it.

I sat up and stretched my arms over my head, and took in the deepest breath of fresh air that I could. Even if the air in my apartment was musty, it was the promise of the day that made it feel like I was breathing in freshness and opportunity.

With the adventures I have planned for today, caffeine was a definite must – but I didn't want just any plain old coffee. The subpar coffee grounds in my cabinet wouldn't do. I had to visit the Sacred Grounds coffee shop right next to the Cozy Cauldron. Their coffee was world famous. Or at least in my opinion it was. I don't know where they get their coffee grounds, but I just knew they had to sprinkle some magic in there.

I didn't make it a habit to go out and get coffee from there very often , so when I did go it was a treat to myself. It was an incentive to get something done. If I had to suffer with cheap coffee every other day of the year, then one night of the year I could splurge on a damn good cup of caffeine.

I put on a simple t-shirt and jeans and made my way out the front door with the biggest smile on my face —more than ready to face the day ahead.

I COULD HAVE MOANED EXTERNALLY, INCREDIBLY LOUD, IF I HAD NO fear of embarrassment or judgment from the people surrounding me in the coffee shop. The vanilla from my cold brew was sweet on my lips, and I had no regrets about my decision to get a five dollar coffee. A thought popped into my head that maybe, just maybe, I could swing by the Cozy Cauldron today and catch a glimpse of Eyden. I don't know why, but my heart craved to see him.

I pushed out the front door and made my across the street, but stopped dead in my tracks when I saw the darkness inside. I checked my watch and realized that it was close to nine in the morning, and he usually didn't open the shop until closer to eleven. I shook my head at the pang of disappointment that shot through my heart, and made my way back towards my own place to get the shop ready for my assistant to open. I would keep an eye on the store until they arrived. I knew it would be a busy day, and I could have easily handled it by myself, but I didn't want to worry about my mortal duties. I wanted the day to be dedicated to me, and who I truly was.

IT WAS TIME.

It was *finally* time.

After helping Holly, my usual seasonal employee, set up the store to open for Halloween night, I made my way back up to my apartment and read *Frankenstein* front to back twice before the sun set and it was my time to shine.

I closed my eyes and dug deep within myself and felt the familiar inkling of my power buried underneath all the crap I covered it with when I wasn't working. The human emotions I allowed myself to feel and the persona I had to wear each and every day. But not tonight.

When I opened my eyes again, and peered into my full length mirror, the ivory of my exposed bones was peering back at me. No more was I covered in flesh and muscle, simply bones. It's why many didn't know that the grim reaper was now a woman. I had no distinguishable features besides my voice, and it was rare that I spoke to a soul before I snatched it. If I did, it was to coax it into my grasp – although many souls were willing to come into my embrace once their time had come and their body expired.

I put on my signature black hooded cloak and disappeared with my scythe like a wraith into the night.

14

EYDEN

Halloween was my favorite day of the year.

Or at least it used to be.

I used to spend my entire night prowling the streets, dressed up with my friends and loving my life. A mountain of candy at the end of the night, and hot chocolate with a scary movie nuzzled next to my mom. It had been her and I for so long, and now it was just me. All alone.

Mind you, I went out on Halloween night until I was a teenager, and then it just turned into buying an excessive amount of candy from the store and eating all of it until my mother and I regretted it in the morning.

And then she died on Halloween, and I could never see myself getting joy from it ever again.

Since she had died I'd spent my time in the store. You never know who might need a good book on Halloween night. Even if it was our slowest day of the year, it gave me something to do. I usually kept the shop open late and read a book because I couldn't face the emptiness of my apartment alone. Alone with the sadness and bitterness in my heart that was there because Death decided to take my mom before I was ready for her to go.

15

KAMARI

62 souls collected tonight.

It always amazed me just how busy Halloween night could be when it came to Death. And just how silly the cause of death could be.

People eating more sugar than they ever had before and dying from it because their bodies couldn't take it.

People who didn't look both ways before crossing the street and getting struck by a car.

People who had heart attacks from haunted houses.

It was sad to think about how fragile the human spirit and life was. It almost made me feel guilty about doing what I did. But it was my job, and one my father had trusted me with when he had passed. If I didn't do it, who else would? It would be anarchy if souls were left to wander, never being ushered to the afterlife.

A sigh escaped my lips as I crossed the street and made my way towards my building. I peered over at the Cozy Cauldron and couldn't help but see Eyden rummaging around the store, as if he was closing shop for the night. I couldn't stop that feeling in my chest again, the fluttering feeling where my heart was supposed to be. If I wasn't in my true form. I'd considered it – but as I was, I decided to stand and watch him for a moment, and as I did so a wave of rightness and peace washed over my body at watching how easily he flowed and ebbed through the shop.

But just as the calmness enveloped my soul, so did panic as the bell in the Common tolled, signaling midnight.

No.

If I didn't make it back to my apartment, very bad things would be coming. I turned from the Cozy Cauldron and did my best to walk in a way that wouldn't attract any attention . There was nobody in the streets, by midnight they were nearly all in their homes taking inventory of their spoils – but regardless I couldn't take the chance.

I wanted to scream curses at the sky when my bones began to glow brightly like a beacon. I had two rules I had to follow with my job. Make it back home before midnight, and don't let anyone see you transform. I knew I'd be breaking one of those rules, but little did I know I'd also simultaneously be breaking the other.

16

EYDEN

I held the keys to the Cozy Cauldron in my hand, having just finished twisting the key in the lock when a bright light from my left caught my attention.

When I turned, I saw a hooded figure glowing. Literally glowing. Bright light escaped every crevice of its clothing, and I couldn't help but be transfixed at what was before me.

What's happening?

I'd seen my fair share of Halloween costumes, and although it had been a while since I'd been out to trick or treat, I knew I had never seen anything like this before. This glowing wasn't intentional. This figure wasn't attempting to draw attention to itself. This glow was otherworldly, and judging by the clothes, the world it hailed from was dark.

Fear settled into my gut as my stellar intuition said that Death itself was before me.

Death was walking the streets of Salem and I should get far, far away from it.

But I couldn't leave, not with what I saw next.

The glowing white light lasted for a minute or two, and

my heart sank as I took in what was before me when the figure disappeared. In the middle of the street, covered in nothing but a black, hooded cloak and carrying a scythe, stood my beautiful girl. The girl who had recently been making my heart flip. The one I had just seen last night and had hoped to see for many more nights in the future. I could tell, even with her back to me, that it was her.

Kamari.

It can't be. Death isn't a person. Death isn't real. Death is a fictional character. A myth.

And I couldn't help the angry words that escaped my lips.

17

KAMARI

"**W**hat the fuck?"

Dread pooled in my belly. I knew that voice surprisingly well for only having heard it a handful of times. But just as I knew, with absolute certainty, that it was well past midnight; I knew that it was Eyden who was standing behind me.

I didn't want to turn around. I didn't want to see the look on his face when his eyes met mine. But I knew I had to. And I knew in my heart that this would be the last time I saw him. The one man I'd ever allowed myself to potentially love. Even if he was a human.

I slowly turned on my heel, making sure I had a strong grip on my cloak so no more of my ivory skin was showing. I already felt self-conscious enough as it was about my current appearance. Usually I was more than happy to parade around in my true form – but in front of him I felt vulnerable. More than that, I felt horrifying.

Seeing Eyden's face made me feel like someone had just ripped my heart out of my chest. I could recognize the fire and the rage within his eyes, but I could also see the hurt, which confused me more than anything. I know it's a shock for a mortal to see a supernatural being, but he didn't look frightened so much as he looked enraged. He looked like he was taking my existence personally.

"Hi, Eyden," I greeted him, trying to keep my voice strong and even, no matter how tough it felt.

"What the hell is going on?" He replied back, his tone icy and leaving no room for pleasantries. It felt like a punch to the gut.

"It's nice to see you too," I replied, trying to lighten the mood with a joking tone, but even with my jovial tone there wasn't a flinch in his facial features. "I was just heading back to my apartment."

"Yeah, I'm sure you were," he said as he crossed his arms over his chest. "So, it's you."

"What do you mean, *it's me*?" I couldn't help the small laugh that escaped my lips. Nothing about this was funny, but it was almost comical that he was acting this way.

"You're the one who took my mother from me."

It wasn't a question, but a statement, and I couldn't stop my heart from plummeting into my stomach. Because there's no way that he could have figured it out. That he knew who I truly was. Besides, how could he possibly know it was me who took his mother's soul? And not my father?

"What are you talking about?" I asked again, trying to keep my voice even.

"Two years ago my mother died of cancer. It was you. It was your fault. You're the one who took her away from me."

"I don't know what you're talking about." I tried to feign innocence, but he's right. It was me. I remember every life I take regardless of how long it's been, or what the cause may be. But I remember his mother so well because she was my first. She was the first soul I ever collected. I remember vividly coming like a thief in the night to await her last breath. Eyden was by her side, holding her hand, his head laid down next to her as he intently listened to her breath and waited for it to stop. I didn't even realize it was him at the time, but now it all made sense. Thinking back on that memory I can see the resemblance. It hurts my soul because I remember feeling his pain. Feeling the strong emotions he felt about his mother and how he stared at his mother's face all the way to the end. I remembered because I found it beautiful. Most humans hide from Death – but he was willing to watch the person he loved most face it head on.

"Eyden..." I couldn't think of any words to say that would make it better.

"You took her from me. You took my world away. She could have survived. She could have made it. But you had to come and take every chance she had." Saliva flew from his mouth as he spit with every word, venom lacing each syllable.

"If you'd just give me a chance to expla—"

"There's nothing that you can say," Eyden yelled, before shaking his head, turning on his heel and walking away. The pain in my chest was unbearable as I watched what I craved for my future walk away – all because I had taken away his past.

18

EYDEN

It felt like I was having a heart attack. Like my heart could explode from all the emotions inside of it.

Rage. Misery. Confusion. Fear.

Rage at Kamari for taking away my mother, and existing in the same town that I had lost her.

Rage; Kamari had taken my mother from me. Misery; Was the one person I had wanted to let into my heart the same being that had caused me the worst pain? Confusion; Why was she in Salem? Why had she made this her home? Fear; Was my life the one she would claim next?

I STAYED INSIDE MY APARTMENT FOR THREE DAYS. I DIDN'T OPEN THE store. I didn't get coffee.

The only things I did were take care of Phoenix and breathe. I could barely take care of myself. I laid in bed and stared at the wall and questioned how my life could be so ironically tragic.

Find a girl I could see myself with? Ends up being the Angel of Darkness.

I felt like I'd swallowed a bitter pill, and even began to question my life choices. Perhaps I would have been happier selling the store and leaving Salem long ago? Maybe that's what I'd do. Get as far away from Kamari, and the bad vibes of this town, as possible. Maybe it's what my mom always intended and would have wanted me to do.

And having these thoughts allowed clarity to consume me.

So that's exactly what I was going to do. But there's one thing stopping me before I go. I finally mustered up enough courage, pulled back the covers, and got my shit together before heading out the front door for my final mission.

19

KAMARI

art of me wondered if maybe I should skip town.
Start all over again and do a much better job of
being the town shut in wherever I ended up next.

I had allowed myself to get too comfortable in Salem.
Too content with spreading my wings and integrating
myself in the town. I'd even used my real name. I thought
the Halloween capital of the world would conceal my iden-
tity, but I couldn't escape my fate. I shouldn't have let the
first town I moved to be the one where I planted my roots. It
was a rookie mistake. My father would be shaking in his
bones.

I'm meant to be alone. I'm not meant to let anyone in.
Maybe I could move to a big city where nobody could tell the
coffee barista from their mailman. Eight million mortals in
the city. I could fit right in. Plus, I'd never allow myself to be
out past midnight again. And if I did, I'd make sure I wasn't
out in the public eye. No matter how secluded I might think
it is.

That settled it. I was moving to New York City. After

nearly a week of wallowing, I would pack my bags and be gone by the next evening.

But part of my soul chipped away thinking about leaving Salem, and my candle shop, behind. Because I had let myself get attached. I had let myself build a life and a routine here. Big mistake. Now that Eyden knew my secret there was no telling what he could do with his anger.

Though, as I went to my front door to answer the adamant knocking, I had a sinking worry that I was about to find out.

I TWISTED THE DOORKNOB AND OPENED MY FRONT DOOR, BUT I couldn't have imagined it would be Eyden standing on the other side. Especially after he'd just found out the worst truth bomb in the entire history of truth bombs.

"Eyden, what are you doing here?"

He looked like he hadn't shaved or brushed his hair all week. He hardly looked like the man I had encountered three days ago. When I peered into his eyes, I could see the anger was still there, but it was being overtaken by sorrow. I wondered if it was more for himself, or his mother. Because there's no way he could be feeling it for me.

"Can I come in?" He asked, the venom finally gone from his words. He just sounded tired. The purple hues under his eyes solidified that fact even more so. I debated with myself on actually letting him inside, but I had no more secrets to hide, and my curiosity always got the best of me.

I wordlessly opened the door further and moved aside to let him in. I usually kept my apartment pretty tidy, but in the panic and mayhem of the last several days, plus my spur of the moment decision to move out of the state, my space was looking like a hurricane had made its way through.

"Nice apartment. Seems very cozy. Especially given your... occupation," Eyden said with a grimace, as if he just realized what he said. "Too soon?" He asked, a tiny smile appearing on his face. I attempted not to look too far into the gesture, or how it made me feel inside.

"I'm not a dark person," I replied. "My occupation may say otherwise, but I didn't choose this. It was passed on to me. I had to play with the cards life dealt me. If I could, I'd buy a cottage as far away from civilization as possible and sell my candles day in and day out. I'd grow a garden, and get some damn chickens or something. The point is, I'd have options and opportunities. It's unfortunate that I'm at the point in my existence where I envy a mortal's life."

"So take your options. Buy your cottage. Live the life you want." He said passionately, and I could tell he was about to hop on his soapbox. "And have all of that with me."

"What? Did you not hear what I said?" I questioned.

"I was pissed at you. Beyond pissed when I found out that you took my mother from me. She was everything I had. But you just told me yourself that you didn't have a choice. I didn't even give you a chance to speak before I stormed away. I let my emotions rule me, and I'm sorry."

"I'm sorry, Eyden. I wish I didn't have to take your mother away. I wish I didn't have to take anyone's mother away. It's not a fun job . If anyone else found out who I was and what I truly do, I could be wiped from existence. Do you understand the type of chaos that would cause the world?"

"So why don't you stop? Can't someone else do it?"

"It's not an option. I wish it was."

"Have you ever even tried?"

"No. Because I know what the answer is going to be."

"You never know what your answer is going to be. You don't know until you actually ask. So ask. Do it for me. Do it for us."

With that, he crashed his lips to mine. I'd kissed were-wolves, vampires, even a couple ghosts. But nothing compared to this. The sparks that flew in my mind. The zing of electricity that traveled from my lips down to my toes. It was single-handedly the best kiss I'd ever had, and when he gently traced his tongue on my bottom lip, silently pleading for entry, I knew I was a goner. I knew without a doubt that this man was for me. That I'd fallen in love with a damn mortal.

He pulled away, resting his forehead on mine, and looked intently into my eyes. I could see my entire future in those eyes.

"Try for me."

I stood, peering into his eyes for a split second before I nodded my head yes. I'd try anything in the world for this man. I'd give up any last sliver of power ever given to me. I'd find a way to make this work. Because I couldn't stand another moment not being with him, and I refused to be the one in charge of taking his soul from him when it was his time.

A genuine, full fledged smile framed his face before his lips were on mine once more, and he made the hundreds of years I'd live worth it. Because I'd finally found the person I could share my own soul with.

THE END

Acknowledgments

I never know what to write in these acknowledgments, but here we are again for the third time in my career.

This story was short and sweet, and I'm so glad you gave it a chance!

As always, thank you to the Lord for giving me the ability to write the stories on my heart.

Thank you to S Frasher & my editor for being the best book baddies ever and making sure this book was ready to go!

I can't wait to be able to write more of Kamari and Eyden following the events of this book!

About the Author

Kylie Vennefron, better known as Ky Venn, loves to build fantasy worlds, and send her characters on great adventures. When she's not writing, you can find her either watching Grey's Anatomy, reading a book, or spending time with her family. She enjoys being a wife, a child of God, and a mama to her daughter and two fur babies. She currently lives with her husband and child in Hamilton, Ohio.

Sign up for my newsletter below for exclusive content, giveaways, sneak peeks and more!

ALSO BY KY VENN

Justice in Magic

Queen of the Sky

Made in the USA
Columbia, SC
14 March 2024